MONSTERS
→ AN OWNER'S GUIDE

About the author and illustrator:

onathan Emmett was an architect before turning his hand
~riting. Since then he has written many books for children, some of
1 have won awards. Jonathan is available in one size only, comes
ready-assembled and does not require batteries.

liver worked as an illustrator in film and television before he started
ng children's books. He has since illustrated books for children of all
and won a few awards too! When Mark was a boy, he morphed
ito a Monster Robot using a large box containing his mum's
new vacuum cleaner. Unfortunately he couldn't bend his
legs and he ended up in the fish pond.

CUSTOMER COPY

~ 004042939 7

DELIVERY NOTE

No 15

SHAMBLES

EXTRAS:

x4

Part no: 15/324

x2

Part no: 15/250

SAFETY CHECKED

REMOVE ALL TRANSIT BOLTS!

A

B

x9

For my own monsters, Max and Laura, who are fully house-trained and will only attack if provoked – J.E.

To Linsay. Fully automated and precisely engineered (no further assembly required) – M.O.

First published 2010 by Macmillan Children's Books
This edition published 2014 by Macmillan Children's Books
a division of Macmillan Publishers Limited
20 New Wharf Road, London N1 9RR
Basingstoke and Oxford
Associated companies throughout the world
www.panmacmillan.com

ISBN: 978-1-4472-3697-9

Text copyright © Jonathan Emmett 2010
Illustrations copyright © Mark Oliver 2010
Moral rights asserted

2 4 6 8 9 7 5 3 1

A CIP catalogue record for this book is available from the British Library.

Printed in China

RECEIVED BY:

HANDLE WITH EXTREME CARE!

MONSTERS
AN OWNER'S GUIDE

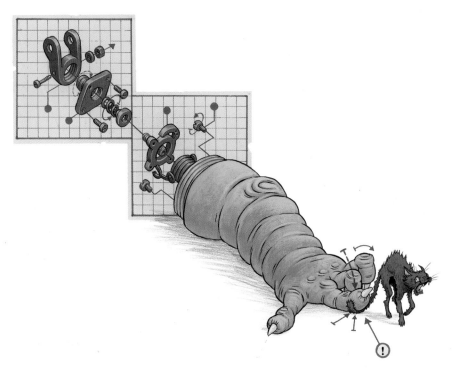

Jonathan Emmett

Illustrated by Mark Oliver

MACMILLAN CHILDREN'S BOOKS

Introduction

Congratulations on your purchase
of a Monstermatic Toy.
A multi-featured creature
that will bring you hours of joy.

This product is designed for use
both indoors and outside.
But before you use your monster,
please take time to read this guide.

Box Contents

The box contains:

1. One owner's guide
2. One Monstermatic head
3. One body
4. Two robotic arms
   (or tentacles instead)
5. Two feet (or hooves)
6. One battery
   (two hundred thousand volts)
7. One screwdriver
8. One allen key
9. Assorted nuts and bolts

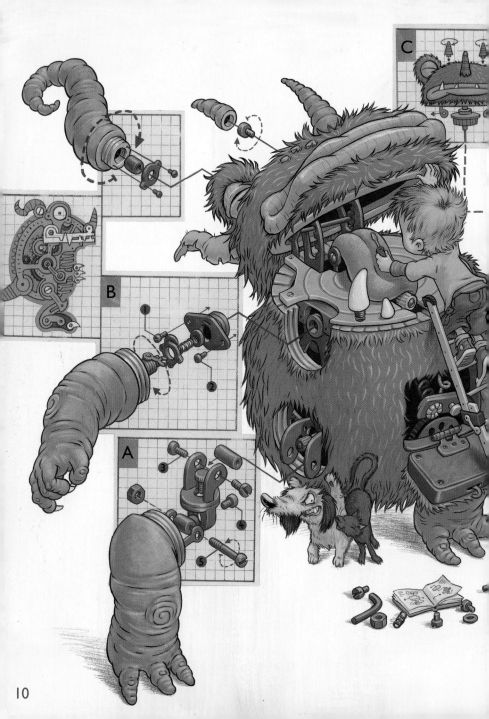

Assembling Your Monster

Bolt legs onto body (as shown in figure A).

Screw in arms (as figure B) and tighten all the way.

Fix head onto shoulders (as figures C to E).

Open chest (as figure F) and insert battery.

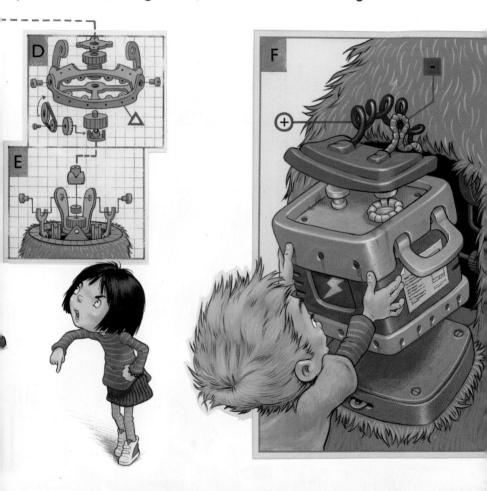

Identify Your Monster

Monstermatic monsters come in many different guise
And their colourings may vary,
as may their shapes and sizes.
This guide applies to every type but,
should you wish to know,
please identify your monster with the diagram below.

No	Pet Name	No	Pet Name
1	Gnasher	10	Moosifer
2	Snook	11	Count Fibula
3	Skulk	12	Emily
4	Beezyblub	13	Dervish
5	Cuddles	14	Shambles
6	Bumfluff	15	Chompski
7	Sark	16	Mister Giggles
8	Banarama	17	Ratchett
9	Oggle	18	Collywobble

Switching Your Monster On

Your monster's power button
is located on its back.
WARNING: ON AWAKENING,
YOUR MONSTER MAY ATTACK!
We suggest you push the button
with a lengthy pole or mast.
And if your monster does attack,
then RUN OFF VERY FAST!

Using Your Monster

Your monster is pre-programmed
and fully automated,
and will make its own decisions
(once its brain has activated).

You may give it an instruction,
for example, "Wash the dishes."
But your monster may ignore you,
and do just as it wishes.

Playing With Pets

Your monster comes complete
with a range of special features,
including the ability to play with other creatures.
Your monster will respond to almost any family pet,
and will only ever eat them
if it sees them as a threat.

Cleaning And Care

Eventually you may feel that
your monster needs a clean.
It may smell of rotten cabbage
and its fur may lose its sheen.
DO NOT TRY TO BATHE IT!
DO NOT SHOWER OR SHAMPOO!
Do not even THINK about it . . .

. . . you'll be sorry if you do.

Dos And Don'ts

- ☑ Do keep your monster happy.
- ☑ Do encourage it to play.
- ☑ Do let it roam around your home.
- ☑ Do keep out of its way.

☒ Don't let it drive a vehicle or use a power tool.

☒ Don't let it play with fire.

☒ DON'T TAKE IT INTO SCHOOL!

⚠️ Safety Information

This product is not
suitable for use with:

Ⓐ chimpanzees

Ⓑ orang-utans

Ⓒ gorillas

Ⓓ or children under three.

This product can be harmful:

Ⓔ If it rolls on you in bed

Ⓕ If it thinks you are its breakfast

Ⓖ If it hits you on the head.

→ Troubleshooting

If your monster eats your family pet
(see earlier in guide):
Open hatch in monster's back
and take pet from inside.

If your monster's on the rampage
and is ransacking your town:
Press and hold the power button
until monster has shut down.

Lifetime Guarantee

We GUARANTEE this monster will cause all kinds of trouble,
will drive your parents crazy and reduce your home to rubble.
And if it ever runs away, gets broken or gets lost,
we'll replace it with a new one — at no additional cost!

№ 25711